To Linda

and the strength of enduring friendships everywhere

—LS

Not So Very Far Away

Written and Illustrated by
LISA SMITH

McArthur & Company
Toronto

First published in Canada in 2004 by
McArthur & Company
322 King St. West, Suite 402
Toronto, Ontario
M5V 1J2

Library and Archives Canada Cataloguing in Publication

Smith, Lisa
Not so very far away / Lisa Smith.

ISBN 1-55278-448-7

I. Title.

PS8637.M565N67 2004   jC813'.6   C2004-903974-1

Jacket and interior illustrations: Lisa Smith

Printed in Canada

The publisher would like to acknowledge the financial support of the
Government of Canada through the
Book Publishing Industry Development Program,
the Canada Council for the Arts, and the Ontario Arts Council
for our publishing activities. We also acknowledge the
Government of Ontario through the
Ontario Media Development Corporation Ontario Book Initiative.

10 9 8 7 6 5 4 3 2 1

Not So Very Far Away

My friend Sarah lives in another city.

She used to live here.

She was so sad to move (and I was sad too).
She left her friends, her relatives and me.

It was hard for Sarah to move to
a new place. It was very far away and
everything was different.

The weather was different,
the school was different, even the
animals were different.

Sarah liked watching birds and
for a long time it was the only thing
about her new home she liked.

She saw familiar birds such as robins,
goldfinches and crows.

She spotted different birds like
magpies and grey jays.

But her favourite bird of all was the little redpoll.

Sarah told me all about the redpolls
whenever we would talk on the phone.

"They're very small birds," she'd say,
"with red caps on their foreheads."

Then she'd try to imitate their song.
"Chet, chet, chet," she'd sing over the line.

The redpolls came to Sarah's
bird feeder every day for sunflower seeds,
and whenever Sarah saw them
she didn't feel so sad.

The tiny birds never stayed still!
They hopped here and there and fluttered
around the feeder like little acrobats.

They always made her smile.

As time went by, Sarah began to feel better in her new home. She started to like going to her new school and playing with her new friends. She got used to snow falling in September.

On weekends, she would hike in the mountains with her mom and dad. She told me all about the bears and golden eagles she'd seen, the thundering waterfalls and the turquoise blue lakes.

Before Sarah knew it, it was spring...

...and one day, much to her dismay,
the redpolls stopped coming to the bird feeder.

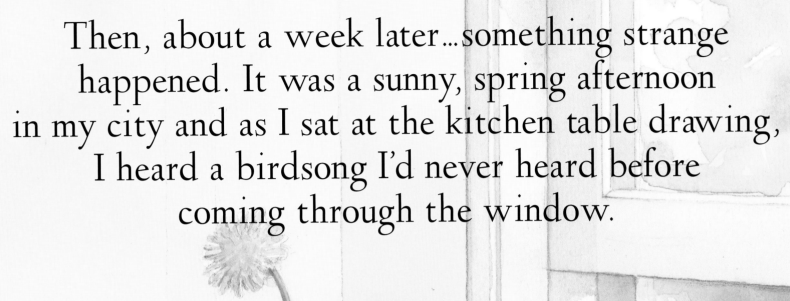

Then, about a week later...something strange happened. It was a sunny, spring afternoon in my city and as I sat at the kitchen table drawing, I heard a birdsong I'd never heard before coming through the window.

I grabbed my binoculars and ran outside.

A flock of little birds was hopping about our cedar hedge singing, "chet, chet, chet"!

They were redpolls!
They even had their little red caps on!

I couldn't believe my eyes.
I was so excited; I wanted to jump up
and down and whoop for joy, but
I didn't want to scare those birds away!

So I just jumped up and down!

I ran inside and called Sarah.
"You sent the redpolls to visit me!"

We laughed and laughed, and somehow Sarah didn't seem so far away any more.

This book is based on a true story. My friend Linda moved to the other side of Canada and really does like to birdwatch. The redpolls came to her bird feeder every day throughout the first winter in her new home and they did appear in my garden for a day, the week after leaving hers. The redpolls have not come back to either of our bird feeders since that time.

Common redpolls are lively little birds in the finch family.
They spend their summers in the Canadian Arctic and winter as far south as southern
Canada and northern parts of the United States in their search for food.
They are sometimes described as accidental, occasional visitors. Redpolls are known for
the bright red caps on their foreheads.

The End